ZERO PHASE

APOLLO 13 ON THE MOON

GERALD BRENNAN

Other titles in the series:

ZERO PHASE

APOLLO 13 ON THE MOON

PART OF THE ALTERED SPACE SERIES

GERALD BRENNAN

TORTOISE BOOKS
CHICAGO, IL

THIRD EDITION, JUNE, 2021

www.tortoisebooks.com

ASIN: B08MBK38Z8
ISBN-10: 0-9986325-0-3
ISBN-13: 978-0-9986325-0-6

Front Cover: Image AS14-66-09272 (NASA/Lunar Planetary Institute)
Back Cover: Image AS14-66-09306 (NASA/Lunar Planetary Institute) Rotated 5º right. Slight airbrushing to expand sun halo.

Helmet and cuff checklist photographs provided through arrangement with the Adler Planetarium. Photo editing for helmet photo by Nick Bianco Photography.

EVA 2   EMU MALF.

ZERO PHASE

APOLLO XIII
ON THE
MOON

PREPARED BY: _____
GERALD BRENNAN

APPROVED BY: _____
R. G. ZEDEKAR

_____
JAMES A. LOVELL
COMMANDER

EGRESS G DEPLOY PHOTO PAN ALSEP ALSEP CONFIG.

PRO. Proceed.

We've been thinking about this for years and simulating it for months and now it's real. 50,000 feet above the surface of the moon. Facing up, looking out the LM windows into blackness. Standing with tension cables clipped to our waists. Gloves and fishbowl helmets on. Flying.

And we've just had ullage and the propellant's settled and the DSKY's flashing 99. Asking us for confirmation. Powered Descent. Program 63. Braking Phase.

I press the button and call it out. "PRO." The button does not fire the engine. "Four." It just tells the computer it's OK to go ahead. "Three." The DPS lights when the AGC wants it to. "Two." We just wait for it. "One."

Freddo calls: "Ignition."

It is not dramatic. Changing numbers on the DSKY and a very slight vibration from the DPS. Not as stressful as, say, a night carrier landing. Or a bad day in the simulator, even.

But it is dramatic. It is real at last. I echo: "Houston, *Aquarius*. We have auto ignition."

For the first 26 seconds, 10% thrust only. The engine needs to gimbal to make sure it's aligned with *Aquarius*'s center of mass. Accelerometers measure vector components along the x, y, and z axes, then give feedback to the computer, which sends adjustments to the engine. Nulling out acceleration along the y and z axes and keeping the thrust vector along the x axis so we don't tumble or spin. Like a toddler wobbling as he finds his balance. But fast. Precise. Automatic feedback loops. A system of systems. Doing it by hand would just foul it up.

Freddo: "Stand by for 26."

"OK, we have throttle up."

94% of rated power. 9,870 pounds of thrust. The whole ignition subroutine is called BURNBABY. This is what passes for humor among computer programmers.

"Houston, *Aquarius*. We are at full throttle." We feel the floor press gently against our feet.

A 2.6-second-delay. We're far enough away that the speed of light makes a difference. And finally, the Capcom's voice: "*Aquarius*, Houston. Roger that."

We're riding the brakes. Orbital Mechanics 101. The descent engine's thrusting in our direction of travel, slowing us down so we can fall out of orbit. The RCS thrusters fire to keep us in line. Inside our fishbowls we hear muffled sounds. Coolant fans, fuel pumps, hisses. Nothing abnormal.

"Landing Radar, Enable." Freddo again. Then: "Jim, give me a two-minute mark."

I watch the DSKY count down the burn time. "And...mark."

"OK. H-dot is low. H is a touch high. Waiting on Noun 69."

"Houston, do we have that?"

The Capcom's voice crackles: "...quarius, Houston. Guidance just sent it up. Minus One-Four-Zero-Zero."

Verb 21, Noun 69. I key in the command. Some programmer at MIT realized years ago that most of our computer commands would be simple sentences. Verb, noun. It was a temporary solution. Six years later, we're flying it to the moon. That's how it is in engineering. The temporary becomes permanent, if it works. Verb, noun. Display angles. Calculate orbit. Fire engine. Here we're adjusting the landing point. A white lie. Kentucky windage. The target hasn't moved. But it's easier to tell the AGC the target's moved than to tell it the spacecraft's out of position.

I hit enter. Accept their adjustment.

Freddo watches the tapes. Compares instruments to printed checklists. At every stage there are indicators of what to do based on the displays, which our controllers are also monitoring in greater detail down in the MOCR. GO or NO GO. (Once we're on the moon, though, it's STAY or NO STAY. When the controllers were writing mission procedures, they realized that once we landed, GO could mean "Go! Launch an abort! Get away from the moon!" or "Go ahead and stay.") Still, if you look close enough, everything in life is a 1 or a 0. Yes or No. Do or Don't.

"Altitude light OFF, Velocity OFF," Freddo calls out. We're getting data from the landing radar, which is behind our backs aimed down. It needs to see the moon. We don't, not yet.

"All right. Verb 06, Noun 63, and the solutions are 800 apart."

Houston: "Not bad, *Aquarius*."

"I'll take it. Verb 57, Enter." We're telling the AGC to accept the radar data. One of the first things you learn as a pilot: trust your instruments. The human body wasn't calibrated for these things. When you're taking off in a jetliner, you can see this. It feels like you're tilted backwards even when you're still rolling along the runway. The otoliths in the vestibular system of the inner ear can't separate acceleration into precise component vectors.

"Let's have a five-minute mark, Jim." Freddo, again.

"And...mark."

"OK. H is 30,750. Only 250 high now."

"OK. Verb 16, Noun 68. We are just over three minutes to pitchover."

Neil said walking on the moon was a 1, on a scale of 1 to 10. All you do is get out of the spacecraft. Walk on the moon. No big deal. He said Powered Descent was an 11. Anyone can walk on the moon. The trick is landing on the moon.

Of course, it hadn't been done before. Landing a manned rocket. They had program alarms all the way down. 1201 and

1202. The rendezvous radar was set to AUTO and ate up too much computing power calculating tracking angles. And they were long on trajectory, so at pitchover everything was unfamiliar. Neil saw the computer was aiming them at a boulder field, so he had to take over. Fly the landing manually. Almost ran out of fuel but he did it. His heart rate was around 150 at landing.

But so far with us, everything's well within norms. We won't see more than a sliver of the moon until pitchover. But if everything looks good, I'll let the computer fly us down.

"Two minutes to pitchover. PGNS to Attitude Hold," I call. A semiautomatic mode. Not quite manual, but close enough to make us feel like we're the ones flying. Here the computer adjusts for all the variables (like sloshing fuel) and holds the LM steady relative to its trajectory. It stays in that attitude until you nudge the stick, and when you let go, it holds the new attitude. A good compromise, given the healthy size of the average astronaut's ego. (I like to think mine's in the lower half of the bell curve. But who knows? Maybe everyone thinks that way.) I give a few quick nudges to make sure it's responding properly in case I do have to fly the landing. "Everything's looking good. Switching back to auto."

"PGNS – AGS is updated," Freddo says. A quick feed of data to the Abort Guidance System, in case we have to abandon the landing approach. But routine. Probably unnecessary today. So far, everything is smooth.

"One minute to pitchover." I call.

"I'm starting the camera."

"30 seconds." We've been memorizing landmarks for months. Or moonmarks, I guess. Patterns of holes. If everything's going as smoothly as the instruments say, I'll see Cone Crater on pitchover.

Freddo: "And we have pitchover."

The LM pivots on its own. Leans forward like a man waking up. We see the eight-balls rolling down in sync like mechanical eyes closing. The lunar horizon rises in our windows and everything is clear and perfect. Beautiful in the moon's stark strange way.

"Houston, *Aquarius*, we have pitchover and Program 64 is running."

For a moment, I'm confused. But the DSKY's given us an LPD angle. 42°. There are sighting marks etched into the windows, and when I look along them at that angle everything becomes familiar in an instant.

"There we are! How 'bout it." I'm excited at last. (We're stuck with mild commentary because the world is theoretically listening. They're probably not, since this isn't the first or even the second landing, but still. Like any publicly-funded institution, NASA has to adhere to a lowest-common-denominator of respectability. Otherwise I'd be tempted to use a profanity or two. Tom Stafford and/or Gene Cernan accidentally let slip a "son of a bitch" during a moment of crisis above the lunar surface on Apollo 10. And I guess you'd say they caught heck for it afterwards.)

"Hot dog!" Freddo's in fine spirits, too. "Right down the line. Outstanding." Of course, this has all been new to him. Even our two Earth orbits prior to TLI.

"This is outstanding!" I echo.

Again I survey the terrain. A dead world. Brownish-gray with sharp shadows. Empty. I was one of the first three human beings to see it up close, back on Apollo 8. One of the first to see the far side, which people mistakenly insist on calling the dark side. The first to take a picture of the earth from the moon.

But there's no time for sightseeing or pondering right now. Without me even needing to ask, Freddo turns back to the instruments. His job title is Lunar Module Pilot. Unless something really goes wrong, he's just calling out information and monitoring the systems. Not as dramatic as command. But obviously still crucial. "2500. Down at 63."

"Roger that."

"2000. Little fast."

"OK." I watch the cross-pointers, scan the other instruments, then look back outside along the LPD angle. Craters getting larger, but it still doesn't look much different. Like parachuting. Until you're really close to the ground, you don't feel all that close. Then it all happens very fast.

"1000."

"Couple little craters. I'm going to redesignate. Two clicks left, one up."

"500 feet, 16 feet per second. Fuel's 11%."

"I'm in Attitude Hold." I've gone to semi-manual controls. I'd wanted to autoland. But better safe than sorry.

"OK. 9% fuel. 250 feet. Looking good. Two feet per second forward, three feet per second down."

"OK, I'm gonna head down." On the console I can see the cross-pointers centered. Stable. Which is what you want on landing. Move too fast laterally on touchdown and you'll tip over.

"150 feet. Descent quantity light."

"Roger that." Under two minutes of fuel left. As expected, but still a concern. And we're in what Neil called the Dead Man's Curve. For most of the descent, we can press a button to abort if the DPS fails. But for about 10 seconds here, we're too low and sinking too fast to pull it off. We'd crash before the ascent engine gave us enough delta-v.

"100 feet." If Freddo's anxious, I can't tell.

"Picking up dust." In this airless place, the scene beneath us hasn't changed in millennia. And now the DPS is blowing moon dust smoothly out in all directions. No clouds, no billows, just streaks heading outward until the dust falls back down. It looks a good bit clearer than the footage we saw from 12. I can see a few craters underneath. And one or two boulders. Rocks in the stream.

"5% fuel."

"Heading down."

"50 feet. Three feet per second. 40 feet. Down at two-and-a-half. We're null on lateral velocity. 20 feet, two feet per second. 10 feet."

There are sensors on strips of foil hanging from the LM footpads. They'll let us know when they're touching the surface so we can manually cut the engine. I wait for it. It is almost done.

Freddo calls "Contact" right when the blue light comes on.

"OK, Engine stop." I mash the button and we fall the last couple of feet and the LM hits with a very slight rattle.

"And we are on the surface!" Freddo claps me on the shoulder.

I nudge the controller so the RCS thrusters stop trying to correct our attitude. "Houston, *Aquarius*, we have a good landing. Very slight plus-Z angle. But we are down."

"Well done, *Aquarius*," they reply at last. "Smooth piece of work."

A few months ago, some journalist pointed out to me that, when we got to the moon, I would undoubtedly be the most travelled human in history. The first man to go into space four times. The first to go to the moon twice. On top of two Gemini flights, the first of which lasted 14 days. If you cracked me open right now and saw an odometer, it would read well over seven million miles. If God sorted the list of *homo sapiens* in rank order by distance travelled, descending, the name at the top would be Lovell, James.

But I'm not dwelling on these things. There's too much work to be done.

Besides, I don't feel different. I'm just a captain responsible for his crew. And that trumps any self-trumpeting. So my next words on this monumental occasion are: "Helium Reg 1 is closed. Talkback is barber pole."

"Recycling the Parker valves," Freddo calls out. "Closed, open, closed, open, open, open, open, open."

"Oxidizer and fuel are gray. Master Arm ON." We're running through the post-landing checklists. Safing the spacecraft and preparing for an emergency liftoff in case something goes really wrong, like the LM starts tipping over or the pressure hull springs a leak after the jolt from the landing. The LM's the flimsiest thing the Grumman Iron Works ever built. The cabin's as thin as three sheets of aluminum foil in places. I know Tom Kelly and his team did a superb job on this thing. It's sturdy enough to get the job done. But you can't take unnecessary chances on top of the necessary ones.

Freddo: "Descent temperature and pressure coming down."

The checklists say we have to prepare for an immediate post-landing abort at T + 1 or T + 2. But I know they'll give us a STAY at both time hacks. Everything has gone incredibly smoothly. Until powered descent I was almost bored. This of course is new, but I've been desensitized by simulations and past missions. I almost have to remind myself it's new. Which is OK with me. A smooth, professional mission to keep the program rolling. The first pure science mission in the program. Apollo 13.

•••

Of course, we are a little late getting to the moon.

We'd been slotted for an April launch. And everything was on track until a couple days before. But Charlie Duke on the backup crew caught German measles from a family member. And Ken Mattingly on my crew had never had it. They said there was a risk he'd get sick while we were on the lunar surface. So there was some noise about breaking up my crew and putting in Jack Swigert from the backup crew as my CMP. And Deke toyed with the idea, I think. Even though no one had ever jumbled up prime and backup crews like that so soon before launch.

Keeping the crew together posed its own problems. We could launch with the slight possibility of a serious medical issue. Or we could wait a month. (Or more precisely, a lunar cycle.) We needed a landing date where the sun angle on our landing site would be about 15^0 over the lunar horizon. So we'd be in bright sunlight but there would be deep long shadows in the craters. Plenty of definition and contrast to help us judge where to set down during the landing. And that meant leaving the Saturn V on the pad four extra weeks and doing another CDDT at the end of it. Figuring out which systems needed to be flushed and purged and re-calibrated.

The systems engineering types around the MSC (usually the ones who came to Apollo by way of the ICBM programs) always talk about tradeoffs. You have to analyze the risk caused by one thing (switching crew members around at the last minute) against the risk caused by something else (keeping a highly sophisticated launch system full of finely-calibrated devices and corrosive propellants out on the pad for an extra month) against the risk of yet another thing (keeping the original launch date and leaving the crew intact and taking a chance on a Command Module Pilot getting sick). Then you make the best decision for achieving your end result. I expected them to take a chance on the first launch window with Ken. Failing that, I figured they'd launch us with Jack in April. But they kept us together and waited.

And the world didn't care.

Not that I expected otherwise, but still. Kennedy's goal had been more than met, so maybe it didn't matter to the public. We hadn't just landed a man on the moon and safely returned him. We'd returned two men safely two times. So when we changed our launch date by a month it didn't even make the front page. My teenage daughter Barbara told me over the phone that we'd been displaced by Paul McCartney's announcement that the Beatles had officially broken up. (I asked her which was more important. She laughed and said, "I dunno, Dad. Launch delays are temporary...") And this was soon overshadowed by far more serious events. Stories of which we were dimly aware, given the intensity of our refresher training, the length of our workdays, and the consequent difficulty of something as simple as relaxing with a newspaper. At the end of April, the U.S. sent forces into Cambodia. A few days later, the National Guard shot four kids at Kent State. A world of uncertainty. As troubled as it had been when we'd first orbited the moon in that lunatic year of 1968.

But here we are. An H-mission. 32 hours on the surface, with Ken orbiting above. Two EVAs and one sleep period. A 2-day, 1-night trip, the travel agent would tell you. Or a .095-day, 0-

night trip, if you're speaking in lunar terms. Getting ready to walk on the moon in the not-so-very merry month of May, 1970.

•••

"And the ICS is PTT..." Freddo says after the T + 2 STAY. PTT is Push-To-Talk—a chance for us to at least work without describing everything to Houston. No time to relax. Always more to do. Checklist after checklist. Everyone wants to walk on the moon. Hardly anyone can keep up with the workload. We're a team of overachievers and we even grumble about it sometimes. I've been so busy I've had to eat and shit at the same time.

"Cabin pressure's good. Pressure regulators A and B on cabin. Cabin gas return is AUTO." Freddo drawls. "HAL still hasn't tried to kill us today."

2001. A favorite of mine. One of those movies everyone talks about, even if they hate it. "Isn't HAL back up on the main ship?" (*Discovery One* in the movie. *Odyssey* for us.) "Suit gas diverter is pushed. Cabin repress is AUTO."

We've been suited up for the whole descent. But since we'll be here for a while, we are closing valves and flipping switches so we can take our helmets and gloves off. Not to relax, just to work a little more comfortably.

"They were all HAL." Freddo points out. He checks the cabin pressure. Then he unlocks his wrists and removes his gloves. (Always the same procedure. Gloves are last on and first off, so you can use your hands for everything else. Probably the same as you'd do if you were bundling up in a snowsuit, only in our case, it's all written down. Documented on official procedure documents with revision dates. Which makes sense, because if we did it wrong, we'd kill ourselves.) "He had eyes everywhere. He killed that one guy with the EVA pod."

"Yeah, I guess he did." My gloves come off and I unlock my goldfish bowl. It's fun doing the simple things in $1/6^{th}$ g. A sudden strangeness to familiar motions. Buoyant and easy without the impracticality of 0 g. I carefully stow my helmet behind us on the ascent engine cover. "I wouldn't mind if ours were that smart. We're more likely to kill ourselves doing something dumb than to be killed by something they did."

"11's AGC almost flew them into a boulder field," Freddo says.

"We could open the wrong valve and the computer couldn't stop us."

"We'd get bored if it was too smart," Freddo points out as he removes his helmet. "This keeps us on our toes."

"It does keep us busy," I acknowledge.

Now we're unhooking the harness and pulley system that lets us fly standing up. A brilliant engineering decision they made back in '62 or so. Low gravity meant we didn't need things aeronautical engineers took for granted on Earth, like seats. No seats meant a lighter LM. And standing put us closer to the windows, which allowed for the same field of view with a smaller window, which meant a lighter LM, still.

We're just about done when there's a crackle. "*Aquarius*, Houston. We're going to need your 047 and 053 values soon."

Freddo keys his mic. "Roger that, Houston. We are back on VOX."

The checklist. There's an undeniable satisfaction to getting it all done. Still, it's relentless.

Freddo keys commands into the DSKY and writes a series of numbers on page 1-1. "047 is plus 37768, 053 is plus 00542."

We've moved on to page 1-2 in the checklist. I call up Program 57 on the DSKY. Lunar surface align.

First we determine the direction and strength of the local gravity vector. If the lander were level and the field of gravity were uniform, it would be straight down. But the moon's not homogenous. Unmixed inside. Say a given area of the surface was stony, but a large nickel meteor struck it eons ago. You'd have a mass concentration. Mascon. These alter the gravitational vector. Plus, the lander's not perfectly level. So what feels like down ends up being something other than straight down from our frame of reference. We need to measure this local direction of gravity more accurately to make liftoff and rendezvous easier. So more work on the DSKY. Calling up angles, displaying angles, measuring the differences between angles, writing down angles. For people like us, it's interesting.

Next up, star alignments using the AOT. (A telescope on top of the LM.) We look through a fixed eyepiece that hangs down like a submarine periscope. It doesn't move, but the telescope up top can rotate into six fixed positions. (Detents, we call them.) You always hear the phrase "pie in the sky." Well, we've sliced the sky into six pieces of pie. So we look at a couple slices of sky and take measurements on our navigation stars. First, I sight Antares, rotating the telescope eyepiece around its longitudinal axis until the star touches a straight baseline on the viewer. Then I write down that angle. Then I rotate the eyepiece again until Antares touches an Archimedean spiral inscribed along with the baseline. Take these sightings on a couple stars, and add in your gravity vector, and you have three vectors that converge on a single point. Enter all this into the DSKY. Noun 79 and Verb 32. And the AGC can do all the rest. This is how you make sure you're oriented properly when you're on the moon.

I'm pretty focused. (No pun intended. Or wait, maybe pun intended.) At least, I'm as engaged as a human being can be when he's slightly tired and his life's no longer in imminent danger. (There was a line in *2001* where HAL says: "I'm putting myself to the fullest possible use, which is all, I think, that any conscious entity can ever hope to do.") Still, I can't help but think back to the Academy. Summers at sea sighting stars with sextants. Other ways to do it down there now, but you still have to learn the basics in case the new ways fail you. And up here, this is the only way to do what we're doing. There are no networks of radio towers or lighthouses to help us plot it out. We're sailors on a strange shore.

• • •

I am not a superstitious man.

In the Navy, there are a lot of arcane rituals. Line crossing ceremonies in the court of King Neptune when you first traverse the Equator, and things of that sort. And superstitions: don't rename a ship, for instance.

Someone around the office—it might have been Buzz, who's obviously not a Navy man, but every bit as anxious as anyone in the Navy or the astronaut corps—asked if I had any qualms about naming my Command Module *Odyssey*. I asked why, and he said *"2001: A Space Odyssey?"* I reminded him that the ship in the movie was called *Discovery One.* He still seemed to think it was a bad omen, but I told him I had no more qualms about it than I had about accepting a mission numbered 13. (And that's about the same level of trepidation I have when a black cat crosses my path. Which is to say, none at all.)

There were a couple odd things about the preparation for this mission. Besides the four-week hold, there was an issue during one of the CDDTs where one of the O2 tanks didn't drain properly. I think we had to turn on a heater and boil off the oxygen inside. And there were a couple oddball simulations while they were trying to keep things interesting for us in the extra month of training, including one where we attempted an abort too late and crashed.

As usual, though, they backed off on the tough sims as our launch date drew near, so we could get some easy wins under our belt and go to the pad confident. So everything seemed pretty stable at the end. Far more so than in the world outside.

I remember checking the weather forecast a couple days before launch. They were predicting hotter temperatures than usual for early May. Florida gets a type of weather called orographic precipitation in May and June and July. It's different than the rain you get in most of the rest of the U.S., which usually comes in on a weather front. In Florida, it's so hot and wet during those months that the moisture evaporates from the ground, from the lakes and swamps and marshes, and by the midafternoon the air's so saturated that it rains like crazy for a good half hour. It happens almost every day, and you can almost set your watch by it.

So I was mildly concerned about weather, but I figured we were launching early enough in the afternoon that we'd be OK. And of course I knew the muggy temperatures wouldn't be a problem on launch day. At least, not for the three of us. When they drive the crews out to the pad, we're always suited up already, with our fishbowls on so we can pre-breathe pure oxygen. I remember seeing beads of sweat on the people waiting to wave goodbye as they walked us outside to the transfer van. Something I hadn't seen on 8, which launched in December. And I saw sweat forming on one technician's brow on the short walk down the metal gantry from the launch pad elevator to the white room where they loaded us into the spacecraft. Meanwhile the three of us were cool and calm in our little cocoons. Pleasantly disconnected from the Florida climate.

Soon enough, Guenter and the pad crew loaded us in to the spacecraft, and we went through all of our pre-launch routines and checklists. And the countdown progressed, and they sealed us up and left, and we worked through still more checks.

Then came launch.

Dramatic, of course, but no major events, nothing at all serious. A pogo vibration on one of the engines during the boost phase, which is where it oscillates along the longitudinal access at a very high frequency due to pressure fluctuations in the combustion chamber. That engine shut down early, but the others burned longer to make up for it. And that was it. Just another trip to the moon.

•••

"*Aquarius*, Houston. Stay! Staaay. Stay! Over." Another decision point after the alignment—STAY/NO STAY for the CSM's first pass since landing. And everything's still routine, so the Capcom—McCandless, now—is being funny.

Freddo and I have a little chuckle. "Houston, *Aquarius*," I respond at last. "I'm not sure if I'm supposed to say 'Roger' or bark like a dog. Over."

"Arf! Arf!" Freddo chimes in.

Nothing. The normal communications delay. The slow speed of light is hell on everyone's comedic timing. "Good LM," McCandless says after a couple seconds.

No one responds. On with the checklist. We're on page 1-7 now. Houston gives us an acquisition time for the CSM to come over the horizon, and we put the computer in P00 mode so they can upload a new state vector. Then on pages 1-8 and 1-9, we have circuit breakers to pull to power down the LM. We switch back to PTT to work.

"I wouldn't mind automating this," I say. The Partial Power-Down checklist shows the proper position for every breaker on Panel 11 and Panel 16. Black dots and white dots. Breakers pushed in, and breakers pulled. Everything already decided, and we just have to do it. "Or the DSKY work. 10,000 keystrokes in the average mission. From a probability standpoint, it's a virtual certainty you're gonna mess up at some point."

"You'll automate us out of a job," Freddo says over his shoulder as he pulls out breakers on Panel 16. He's a great pilot and a sharp guy, an ex-Marine from Mississippi, the first in his astronaut class to get up here. But by now everyone knows Apollo won't last forever. A lot of great pilots won't fly again. "I know you're retiring after this, but the rest of us still need to work."

We finish with the breakers and move on to 1-10 and 1-11 to confirm switch settings on the front panels.

"They're still gonna send people up here." I tell him. "No one cares if a robot sees the whole earth. No one cares if a computer's taking a chance on not coming home. People only care if something can happen to them."

"The average Joe is starting to know this can't happen to them," Freddo says, with a nod that says he means the mission, the moon, everything. "All right, Houston, Partial Power-Down complete, and we're back on VOX."

I can't argue with Freddo. Someday, maybe, but no time soon. For me, the most compelling thing about *2001* was the notion that someone could someday just buy a Pan Am ticket and fly to the moon. But would people still want to go, if it were that easy? There's not much here. It might end up one of those places everyone theoretically *could* go to, but nobody does. Like Greenland, or Antarctica.

"All right, *Aquarius*, we have an estimated P22 time of 110 plus 48 plus 00."

"Roger that, Houston."

"And we've completed our data upload, so the computer's yours."

"OK, Houston. We are ready to go with our terrain description." The next item on the checklist. We have to describe in detail everything we see through the LM windows. Given the fact that we'll be walking around out there soon enough, it might not seem like a productive way to spend our time on the surface. But a job's a job. And it'll help refine our plans for the EVAs.

"*Aquarius*, Houston, go ahead with your description."

"Terrain is relatively uneven. More so than we expected. Maybe five- to ten-meter rises. There's one about 30 meters to our north and another to our south further away. It's almost like a series of sand dunes, although obviously these were formed differently. Not as many rocks as expected. We can only see about a dozen boulders that are larger than a foot in diameter."

Freddo has taken out the 70mm Hasselblad and is shooting pictures out the right window.

"We saw the Doublet coming in, and we should be able to set up the ALSEP nearby." (The main task for today's moonwalk—an experiment package. I'm more excited about tomorrow's EVA. We're walking a mile east to Cone Crater. 1,000 feet wide, 750 feet deep. It should be quite a sight. And a great site for some geology fieldwork. Still, today should be fun. A walk on the moon is a walk on the moon.) "The color varies depending on how close you are to zero phase. It's more brownish when you're looking off to the side. Down-sun, things get pretty washed-out."

We continue with the descriptions. Obviously we'll be able to see more once we're out and about. But this is on the checklist, so it's a point of pride to do as good a job as possible. And we've been practicing, too. Field trips with Lee Silver from Caltech in the Orocopia Mountains. Going around a bend, then calling back on a walkie-talkie. Fast, accurate descriptions. No more words than necessary.

After a while, Houston interrupts to give us an update on consumables. RCS fuel, oxygen, water, electricity. And they send liftoff times for Revs 16, 17 and 18. (Like everything else, our communications are incredibly complex. As the earth turns above us, various stations around the globe fall out of line-of-sight, and others come over the horizon. California, Australia, Spain. These retransmit our voices to the MOCR in Houston. If something happens and we can't re-establish communications within a set time, we'll need the liftoff times handy to rendezvous with the CSM. You might think they'd transmit them up directly to the computer, but it's all pen and notepad.)

It's only now that I realize how hungry I am. One of those sudden hungers that hides until it's too big to miss. But we're not far enough on the checklist. An erasable memory dump, and a check on our actual landing location versus the plan, and some more circuit breaker configuration changes.

"And our status report is as follows: We've taken no medication," I report at last. "We're both in excellent shape. Commander's PRD is at 15953, and for the LMP is 09392." (Dosimeters. We'll get the equivalent of several chest x-rays worth of radiation on this trip.)

"Roger that, *Aquarius*. 19953 Commander, 09392 LMP." McCandless reads back. "You in the mood for some food yet?"

"We are getting pretty hungry, Houston. I was thinking of ordering Chinese."

A pause. A chuckle. "Uhh, we'll try to get the delivery guy in the simulator as soon as possible. I don't think we can have him up there today, though."

"All right, I guess we'll eat what we've got. And we are going to PTT." To Freddo, I ask: "What's on the menu, anyway?" Back at Annapolis, my fellow plebes and I had to memorize the menus and recite them to any upperclassman who asked during the course of the school day. And of course, as upperclassmen, we got to ask the plebes. Obviously Freddo and I are on a fairly equal footing here. Still I can't help thinking about that.

"Beef sandwiches, carrots, strawberry cubes." Freddo distributes out the packs.

"Mmmm. Strawberry cubes." And the sandwiches all freeze-dried and wrapped up in plastic and covered in gelatin so we don't get crumbs everywhere. I'm remembering the scene in *2001* where they're riding the lunar shuttle. Pulling out lunch, oblivious to the alien scenery. Making mild jokes about bland prepackaged sandwiches. Still I'm eager to eat. Hunger is the best sauce.

"Just like mom used to make," Freddo says as he digs in.

"I'll tell you, it's still a step up from Gemini."

"I bet. Probably a lot less cramped, too," Freddo says between chews.

"This thing feels like the Waldorf compared to Gemini." I look around. There's always been an unfinished feel to the LM interior. Like a ship's engine room. Gray bulkheads and exposed wiring. But far roomier than Gemini. We even have hammocks for our sleep period. "Tom Stafford said Gemini was like eating, sleeping, working and shitting while stuffed into the front seat of a sports car wearing an overcoat."

"And you had two weeks of that with Frank Borman sitting next to you."

I chuckle. "Frank's all right. Helluva pilot. Just about the most decisive man I've ever met. I'm probably the only guy that could put up with him for two weeks, but he's all right." I eat my so-called sandwich. "We pranked him in orbit. Gemini 6 and 7, we were up there for our rendezvous not too long after the Army Navy game. And between our two missions, Wally and Tom and I realized it was three Annapolis grads and a West Pointer. So after we rendezvoused we were floating nose to nose with them. All part of the flight plan. And they radioed over saying they had a visual acuity test for us. And we looked out the portholes. And they'd put signs over their windows. GO NAVY. BEAT ARMY."

Freddo snorts. "What'd Frank do?"

"He just got all gruff. Said it was a bunch of crap, and asked why were we wasting time with it. Great pilot, sharp engineer, lousy comedian," I reminisce. "That was a rough two weeks, though. Once all the fun stuff was done, we were reading to pass the time. Reading. In space. It was just that boring. On 12, with Buzz, we at least had a tighter schedule. But on 7...you'd never think space travel could get boring..."

"*Aquarius*, Houston." Again, the radio. "We have an update on your location. Based on your crater descriptions, we think you're at Charlie Quebec 0.6, 65.5. Over."

"Roger, Houston. I copy Charlie Quebec 0.6, 65.5." I wolf down a few bites of sandwich so I can scribble it down. We've planned our traverses on the surface using photographic maps from the earlier missions, and we need this information to navigate once we're out there.

Back to the meal. We finish in hurried silence. Scarfing down mediocre food because we've got a lot to do before we can eat again. On Gemini 7, once the rendezvous with 6 was over, we were going for endurance, so we got bored. 12 kept us much busier. On Apollo 8, I was back with Frank, who was good at pushing back against the bureaucracy just enough that our schedule didn't get too cluttered. And now this feels like a total race against the clock. At least here on the surface. Maybe that's the overall trend. More bureaucracy means more managers and scientists trying to squeeze items onto the checklist. And that means more work. Which makes sense. If an institution spends $375 million on a mission and puts three men in harm's way, it wants to get its money's worth. A natural trend. Something some of the Original

Seven didn't understand. Some of them tried to buck it, and now they're not astronauts any more.

When I saw *2001*, I thought of Gemini 7. At least in that part of the movie when they first show the astronauts on *Discovery*. Listless, playing chess. Eating, unexcited. Watching news bulletins with dead eyes. Bored. Now that we're so busy, I am a little jealous. Lord knows I don't mind the work, but I'd also like to at least relax while we eat. Maybe that's just how it is, though. When you have one thing, you want the other.

●●●

Not only am I not superstitious, I am not an overly religious man. Which isn't to say I equate religion and superstition. We go to church regularly. And everyone knows we read from Genesis back on Apollo 8. It seemed appropriate, and everybody but Madalyn Murray O'Hair seemed to like it, but I have to admit it was Frank's idea. So I'm not as religiously religious as some people in the astronaut office. But there are some on the other side of the scale, too. Atheists, agnostics, freethinkers. Which is all well and good. It takes all kinds.

My father passed away when I was 12. Mom had to raise me by herself. We lived in a one-bedroom apartment. That's just how it was.

I guess what I'm trying to say is this: I had to work for everything I got. They say your father is your first image of God. Mine was there, and then he wasn't.

I know a couple guys that pray during every flight. And Gene Kranz prays before every shift in the MOCR. I don't know that

I've ever done anything like that. Not that I'm morally opposed, but it seems counterproductive. A distraction from the work. God helps those who help themselves.

•••

And now it's time to walk on the moon.

Almost time, I should say. It's time to get ready, at least.

EVA, as you might imagine, requires a very lengthy checklist. You have to put everything in its right place before you start so you can reach it when you need it. And you have to do everything in the right sequence so there's a minimum of wasted effort. (For instance, we unlock the front hatch before we put our gloves on. It sounds dangerous, especially since the hatch is so thin it bulges outward when the LM's pressurized. But with an inward-opening hatch and 5 psi inside, there's no risk of it coming open before we bleed off the cabin pressure, and it's much easier to unlatch it in bare hands.) It's times like this that the checklist is a lifesaver, literally and figuratively.

In the prep phase, I pulled out our little portable magnetic tape player, and now we're listening to that while we get everything in place. Boots, gloves, LEVA helmets (the over-helmets with the gold visor that we wear over the fishbowls), PLSS packs, RCU units. And all the while, music. First the theme from *2001* and then that *Age of Aquarius* song. Not so loud as to get in the way if Houston calls. Just enough to get excited.

When we're getting our LEVA helmets out of their bags, we each find letters from our wives. A wonderful touch. Unexpected. Apparently they'd arranged it with Deke, who'd talked to the right people to sneak them in there during the final LM closeout and put them where we wouldn't see them until we were on the moon. On Apollo 8, once we realized we'd be gone for Christmas, I'd arranged for a surprise for Marilyn. And now apparently she wanted to do something special for me. I won't go into the contents, but it's a very nice surprise.

And now, back to the nitty gritty. Filling drink bags so we'll have water during our four-and-a-half hours outside. (A new enhancement. They didn't have them on 12, and they got very thirsty.) Emptying our urine bags so they won't overflow. Heads out of the metaphorical clouds and back on the lunar ground.

• • •

I should mention that I'm by no means special in my capacity for hard work. That's the thing about Apollo. You see so many people giving 120% every day for years on end, and you feel like a slacker if you're just at 110%.

So this is a team effort, a tremendously dedicated team of very smart people working very long hours in very disparate locations. Flight controllers in Houston. Pad workers at the Cape. Contractors at Grumman and North American in Long Island and southern California. Subcontractors at Beech Aircraft and Eagle-Picher and MIT and a thousand other places. We've spent years not only training and working and planning, but visiting factories, talking to workers who are working every bit as hard as we are but who will never be in the public eye.

It motivates both ways.

We are reminded again and again that we're part of something much larger than ourselves. An organization of tens of thousands. A living breathing thing that learns and adapts from mission to mission. A team of teams that, despite some fits and starts, is now hitting its stride. Turning something into reality that's been a dream since man first looked up at the sky.

Meanwhile they get to see that there's a living breathing human being whose life depends on their handiwork. They get to shake our hands and look us in the eye. And once you've looked a man in the eye and you know that his life depends on you, say, getting a weld right or sealing a window properly, you tend to take your work a little more seriously.

At least, that's the theory.

They say practice makes perfect, but only theory's perfect. Practice can't be. Is it possible to create a system with millions of components, then assemble and use them so perfectly that nothing will fail? No. If we made all 6.5 million components with a 99.9% reliability rate, we'd still have 6,500 failures.

The Fire was a big motivator, in its own sad way. We lost three great men. Ed White, in particular, was one of my closest friends in the astronaut office. After that everyone realized that, no, we were not going to skate by on luck or Divine Providence or whatever, and that good men not only could die but had, in fact, died. Everyone buckled down and took everything even more seriously after that. Still, it's statistically certain that some things will go wrong. Like the pogo vibration.

So it's been obvious for a while that it won't be perfect. But we're not gonna stop trying.

Given all the brainpower involved, there's been a lot of effort towards figuring out ahead of time where things will go wrong. The systems engineers tend to do this using probability trees. Basically you sketch out a series of events that has to happen, and each failure mode is a branch splitting off. So if you're, say, starting your car, and you know the ignition system works a certain percentage of the time, and you know each sparkplug fires a certain percentage of the time, and the fuel pumps pump correctly a certain percentage of the time, and so on and so forth, you can sketch it out and figure out the overall percentage of times the car will start, and see if you're OK with that. And if you're not, you can add redundancy in some areas and try to get the overall percentages up. Not everywhere—you wouldn't want to install a second engine, for instance. But usually you can make the main branches thick enough and sturdy enough to get you where you want to go.

At least on paper.

•••

About midway through the EVA procedure, we realize we're alone. No communication with Houston. We're cut off from humanity. Talking to ourselves. A quarter of a million miles away from any human who isn't named Ken Mattingly.

"Houston, *Aquarius*, how do you read, over?" Freddo calls. We wait. No answer. We wait a few seconds more. Nothing. "Jim, do you have comms on your PLSS?"

"Houston, *Aquarius*, how do you read?" I try. "No, no comms." We have to iron that out. We can't go outside if we can't talk to each other. We can't stay on the moon if we can't talk to Houston. "I'll switch back to ship's comm." I cycle the breaker and flip a switch. "Houston, this is *Aquarius*, do you read, over?"

A pause. The comm delays are bad for comedy but good for dramatic effect.

And then: "*Aquarius*, Houston. You're still there?"

"Roger that, Houston. We seem to have lost comm on the PLSSs. Let's sync up and try to work through it, over."

"OK. Stand by one while we talk procedure down here."

"OK, Houston." We wait. You might think we'd have been panicking already, but that never helps you solve a problem. Especially not up here. The overly emotional types don't succeed as pilots, let alone astronauts. And the first rule of spaceflight is: If you don't know what to do, don't do anything. You just have to take a breath and think through it. Work the problem.

"*Aquarius*, Houston. We're going to have you go back to the beginning of the PLSS comm check block on the EVA-1 card and verify your switches."

"OK, Houston. Back to the PLSS comm check block." A normal problem-solving technique in spaceflight. When something's wrong, you go back to the last point in the checklist where everything was right and set your switches back to what they were. Then work through it again, more methodically.

Another *2001* line comes to mind—Hal saying "This sort of thing has happened before, and it's always been due to human error."

"*Aquarius*, first, did you unstow your PLSS antenna?"

"Yes, we did, Houston."

"OK, back we go, then."

The checklist cards are hole-punched and held together with ring clips. Like you'd buy at an office supply store. The assemblage hangs from toggle switches on the instrument panel so we can see them while we work. I grab it and flip back to the right spot, and Houston confirms our breaker positions, and then we proceed to test the comms.

After fifteen minutes, we find the culprit. An audio circuit breaker on my panel that was left out after we cycled them earlier. A glitch in the checklist, which wasn't completely explicit. I make a mental note to mention it in the postflight debriefing so they can fix it for 14.

Then we continue. Making sure we're ready to go outside. Like getting bundled up for an unbelievably bad snowstorm, with a room full of anxious mothers monitoring your every move. Connecting O2 hoses from the PLSSs to the ports on our chest. Donning our helmets. Making sure everything is locked on. Then making sure the locks are locked.

We are moving to page 2-9. I grab for the checklist and miss. It comes off the toggle switches easily in $1/6^{th}$ gravity and falls very gently to the floor.

Freddo and I make a move for them at the same time and then stop. I have a brief awful vision of us somehow banging our helmeted heads so hard we crack one of the fishbowls. An ignominious end to the mission. We'd have to call off the EVA. Leave the moon without going outside. Hear about it for the rest of our lives.

"We almost pulled a Three Stooges there," I say.

"Two Stooges, one in orbit," Freddo observes. (We're on a different frequency than the CSM for now, so Ken doesn't get to listen or respond, but I can almost hear him saying "Speak for yourself, *Aquarius*.")

"All right *Aquarius*, let us know when you've got your gloves on," Houston says.

As I mentioned, the gloves are just about the last step before going outside. We are almost there.

• • •

I was building and flying rockets when I was 12 years old. Poring through Chesley Bonestell illustrations before anyone knew we'd be able to see these things for real. When I was a midshipman, I wrote my thesis on rocketry. I remember reading von Braun's features in *Collier's* at around that same time. When Neil Armstrong and Buzz Aldrin were still flying fighters in Korea, I already wanted something bigger.

And now it's all happening. Years of hazy dreams compressed by hard work into hours of dense fantastic reality.

• • •

"*Aquarius*, this is Houston. You are go for cabin depress."

"OK. Circuit breaker, cabin repress open." We are setting the environmental system so it won't try to repressurize the LM once we dump the O2. "Cabin repress valve closed."

"Roger that, *Aquarius*."

I reach for the overhead dump lever. It's painted black and yellow so you know it's important. I pull it and hold until the cabin pressure goes down to 3.5 psi. Then we monitor the gauges on our RCUs to make sure our suits are holding a higher pressure.

"4.8," Freddo calls out.

"4.9 and coming down," I echo. The suits are designed to run at 3.8. We wait until the gauges settle there before finishing the cabin dump. "Holding at 3.8," I call out at last.

"3.8," Freddo echoes.

"OK, give us a mark for the final depress so we can start our watches," Houston says.

My hand goes back to the overhead valve. "Three, two, one, mark."

I pull it open again. The EVA has officially started.

After two minutes, the internal pressure's below 0.1 psi. Low enough to open the front hatch. My suit pressure has spiked again in response to the pressure drop outside, so when I first reach for the handle I feel like the Michelin man.

"Puffed up here. When it comes down I'll open the hatch."

"I'll get the PLSS feed valves open," Freddo says. We're wearing water-cooled underwear. Laced with tiny tubes that cycle to a sublimator on the PLSS, which carries off the residual heat. The valves are tricky to reach on your own, so we help each other out. "OK. Caution and warning status is good. Water SEP light, pre-amps, ECS."

"OK, water flags are clear," McCandless calls out.

The suit pressure's back down and mobility's back up. Time to get out. I swing the hatch the rest of the way open while Freddo dims the lights.

I turn left and kneel. To get out, you have to basically slither feet-first out the open hatch on hands and knees. The LM is a tight squeeze and this is the tightest thing we do. I have to be careful not to scrape my faceplate on the midstep. Freddo guides me and holds my antenna so it doesn't snap off. I can feel the hatch frame through my suit. Stopping me. Then Freddo guides my PLSS to drop it a little and I remember to arch my back like in training.

With that, I'm through.

There's a small metal porch outside, and once I'm through the hatch, I'm on it, still crawling backwards. "OK, I'm clear."

"Stand by for the jettison bag." Through the hatch I can see Freddo moving over to my side of the LM. The bag's a big white beta cloth thing full of trash we don't want to haul back into orbit later. Just about the size of a head and torso. Freddo works it through the hatch.

I grab it and drop it overboard. "All those years in Boy Scouts, I feel like I'm littering."

"Don't worry about littering," Freddo drawls. "Unless a park ranger shows up to chew us out."

Next Freddo passes out the LEC, which is basically a clothesline-type conveyor belt device which we'll use to haul the rock boxes back up into the LM.

At last I pull the D-ring to deploy the MESA platform.

"OK, we have you on camera," Houston calls.

There's a pleasant lightness to my body as I swing my legs down. I'm in the shadow of the LM but I can see very well, thanks to the surface backscatter.

"Looking good. We see you coming down the ladder." Houston again. "The stripes were a great idea." (After 11 and 12, they couldn't tell who was who in half the pictures. So my suit has red armbands and leg bands, and my LEVA has a wide red stripe down the middle. And I took the liberty of having them add a blue anchor insignia to it.)

The LM footpads look like big dinner plates wrapped in gold tinfoil. Right now I can't see the one beneath me. My RCU is in the way. But assuming the landing struts haven't compressed, I know the footpad is about a yard below the ladder's bottom rung. We have to go down the ladder by feel. As I do, it occurs to me I haven't decided what to say when I set foot on the moon.

"It might be a little dustier than we've seen in the past," I say after I hop down to the footpad. "The footpads look like they're a couple inches in." I hop back up to make sure I can get back to the bottom rung of the ladder. Despite the distance, it's an easy jump. "Mobility is fine. And I'm ready to step off the LM."

I step off.

"*Ex Luna Scientia.*" (Our mission's motto. Inspired by the Naval Academy's: *Ex Scientia Tridens.*) "From the moon, knowledge. The first pure science mission in Apollo, and our first round of exploration is under way." Apollo 11 was about learning to land on the moon. Apollo 12 was about learning to land accurately. And now that we can do both of those things, it's time to get some work done. Targeted landings close to important geological—or rather, selenological—features. Real science.

The surface checklist, which is mounted on my wrist, says to spend a couple minutes getting used to the lunar gravity. Learning to walk anew. (We've practiced a little, back in the Vomit Comet, so it's somewhat familiar.) There are a few methods: kangaroo hop, skip, slow stride. It isn't physically hard, but your body feels so buoyant that it almost gets away from you. (It occurs to me this is something they got wrong in *2001.* They did an incredible job filming the 0 g scenes and the artificial gravity scenes on the ship. But in the lunar scenes, everyone's walking normally.)

At last, I get a good look around. There are some very light radial streaks from the descent engine etched in the gray lunar soil. Other than that, everything's pristine. Like a new snowfall. Leaving footprints makes you feel both guilty and gleeful. But the moon's rough, too. So more like a beach or a desert. Bright sun, black sky. No stars as long as the gold LEVA visor's down. Strange and inviting and new. Nothing man-made but the LM. Aluminum and fake gold Mylar.

"Jim, you look like you're having a blast out there," Fred says.

"It's like bouncing on a trampoline. Except I'm all bundled up." It is neat. But also time to get back to business. "Mobility is good. The LM struts are evenly depressed. It seems we landed on a forward slope." Still, I can't resist one last little bit of fun, as the first Annapolis grad on the moon. "Also, somebody tell Buzz the Army-Navy game is now tied at one."

Another chuckle from Mission Control. "OK, Jim, we'll pass that along."

●●●

Houston does at least understand that we're busy. That there are certain things we have to do and other things that will just get squeezed in when we can get to them. We only talk to the Capcom, who's always a fellow astronaut. But officially the flight director on shift (Kranz, Griffin, Frank or Windler) is in charge of the overall mission. I'm in charge of the spacecraft, but we have to listen to Flight. Chris Kraft, the original, wrote something into the rulebook a while back: The flight director may, after analysis of the flight, take any action necessary for the successful completion of the mission.

Now obviously, they're not up here to make us do anything. So there have been pissing matches here and there between astronauts and controllers. And that tends to be bad for the astronaut's career. But most of us are team players, and by and large we work extremely well together. And there's an unspoken acknowledgement that we'll make a good faith effort to get everything done, and they won't press us unless something's absolutely crucial.

A lot of tasks fall into a middle ground. Like stirring the cryo tanks on the CSM, which Ken has to do periodically. Otherwise they separate into layers and the ground has a hard time taking accurate measurements of our liquid oxygen, hydrogen and helium. And of course, without accurate measurements, you can't make sound decisions. There's a general schedule to things like the cryo stir, but if other things pile up and it happens an hour later, no one minds. Normally it isn't a problem. Just another task on the list.

• • •

Our first indication something's wrong happens when I've been outside for about 15 minutes.

"*Aquarius*, Houston. We need to hold off on the two-man EVA, over," the Capcom says.

"Copy, Houston." Fred sounds unperturbed.

Per the checklist, I've retrieved the 70mm Hasselblad from the transfer bag. The scenery's gotten a little boring now that I've been outside a few minutes. It's hilly but by no means rugged. Nothing as jagged as Bonestell painted, although the adrenalin of actually being here makes up a lot of the difference. Magnificent desolation, Buzz said on 11, and that sounds about right. (I'm hoping we'll see some nice panoramas once we're at a higher elevation.) I can see Fred through the window, finishing up some circuit breaker changes.

"OK, Houston, we are standing by," I add. I look around again. You can see long shadows looking up-sun, but it gets incredibly bright, even with the visor. And down-sun, the closer you get to zero phase, the more boring it looks. All washed out. You get a lot of backscatter. And finally all shadows are hidden by the objects that cast them, with only your own to relieve the blandness.

"Uhh...Jim, we're working through a comm problem with *Odyssey*." The Capcom sounds distracted. "Possibly a telemetry issue. In the meantime, we'd like you to go ahead and grab the contingency sample."

This is a quick scoop of lunar soil. We're always supposed to grab one soon after landing in case we have to lift off early. We practice for every contingency. And normally the contingency sample is just that. But something about McCandless's tone is off.

I get the sample scoop from the MESA and grab a loose pile of soil.

"Houston, I'm picking up a sample about 100 feet from the LM at the 11 o'clock position."

"Uhh, roger, Jim," McCandless replies. More delay than normal.

My sample goes in an airtight plastic bag. The entire landscape's a bleak panorama of grey and beige. But up close the soil appears black as coal. I'm standing on the moon and I still can't tell what color it is.

"OK, Houston, I'll get started on pictures," I add. I'm supposed to take a 360⁰ panorama, so I start snapping. I can remember family vacations where I wasted time taking pictures and got home and everything looked flat and boring, because I was no longer there, no longer feeling that excitement. I'm wondering if that will happen here.

"*Aquarius*, we won't have time for that," McCandless replies. "Jim, we need you to get back in the LM."

"Roger, Houston. Do we have a timeframe for resuming EVA, over?"

"Jim, we've had a problem with *Odyssey*. We need to do an off-nominal closeout and a liftoff and rendezvous on Rev 18. Please acknowledge, over."

My heart sinks.

When my late, great friend Ed White did America's first EVA back on Gemini 4, they had to call him back inside once the spacecraft was nearing orbital night. Glorious panoramas, floating free in space—and then back in the tin can with the tiny window, wondering if you'll ever be out there to see it again. Ed was a dedicated astronaut, a West Pointer and an Air Force major, devoted and disciplined. And when they summoned him back inside he said: "This is the saddest moment of my life."

This is the first thing that flashes through my mind. Ed wouldn't make it back up there, but he didn't know it. I know I'll never be back.

Then: This must be serious.

"Roger, Houston. Liftoff on Rev 18."

Just under two hours away. But I can't stay outside. There is work to be done.

I bound back to the LM and put the camera back in the transfer bag for Freddo to haul it in. "Any details on the problem, Houston?"

"Jim, we had Ken do a cryo stir and he heard a bang. Comm dropped briefly. Now we're back up, but the O2 Tank 2 pressure is off-scale low. He had a main bus undervolt and a couple fuel cells dropped off. And he's having problems stabilizing the spacecraft."

"Roger, Houston. How soon can I talk to him?"

"Jim, he's almost overhead, but we'll lose VHF line-of-sight in a few minutes. We're gonna set you up on the S-band once you're in the LM."

"Roger, Houston. Heading inside." I take a few quick swipes at my moon suit, which has barely had time to get dirty. And I realize I haven't looked up at the earth from out here. It seems stupid to stop for that, but something tells me I should. I know it's high, almost vertical. I grab the ladder and crane my head back and there it is. Far more beautiful than the moon from the earth. Round and inviting. Everything. I only allow myself a brief glance.

Then: a smudge in the sky. Far closer than Earth, straight above, moving fast like a meteor.

"Oh, Christ." I get a cold black feeling in the pit of my stomach.

"Say again, Jim," Houston says, but I'm already swiveling to try and see the CSM again before it passes over the horizon.

"Houston, I caught sight of *Odyssey* on this pass. And it seemed to be surrounded by...a cloud of some sort."

"Jim, Ken said he was seeing gas and debris outside the window."

"But you still have comm."

"Roger, Jim, the CSM Capcom is talking to him right now."

"Do we have a revised checklist for end of EVA so I can get on there?"

"We'll make some adjustments and get you up on the S-band right away. Then we'll circle back."

Freddo interjects: "We'll do a rapid version of the rapid closeout. Just dust off your suit and throw away the LEC on your way in."

I respond: "I'm already cleaned up."

I have my hands on the handrails and I've already taken the short fateful hop to the bottom rung. I've taken my last footsteps on the moon. I don't care anymore.

• • •

The CSM orbits the moon every two hours, give or take. Our trajectories on the way out always aim for a spot just ahead of the leading edge of the moon. (The left, if you're looking from the Northern Hemisphere.) And that determines the plane and direction of the CSM's orbit. It always disappears over our western horizon (the direction of the LM windows) and reappears to the east, behind us.

48 minutes of its orbit is spent in complete communications blackout, with the bulk of the moon blocking radio transmissions to and from Earth, and keeping us from communicating with them as well.

Right now we have a brief window where we could talk directly to Ken on the VHF, but it'll only last until the CSM goes below the lunar horizon. About six and a half minutes from when *Odyssey* was directly overhead. With the S-band, our words have to go from moon to Earth and back, so there's more delay. But we'll be able to talk until Ken passes behind the moon.

●●●

Ordinarily once I'm inside the LM, we'd get ourselves on *Aquarius*'s oxygen and repressurize. But I'm barely through the hatch when Fred starts reconfiguring circuit breakers to get us back on the S-band. The normal checklist has gone out the window.

Soon, we're up. "*Odyssey, Aquarius.* How do you read, over?"

Nothing.

Again, I call: "Ken, this is Jim. How do you read, over?"

A long pause. About five seconds. The laws of physics refuse to bend to our urgency.

At last: "Clear enough, Jim."

"All right, Ken, what's the situation?"

I wait.

Then: "Jim, there appears to be a cloud of debris around me. O2 Tank 2 is still off-scale low. I think it exploded during the cryo stir."

"What are the levels on Tank 1?" The tanks are next to one another. Which is obviously bad. Everything's been designed with a certain percentage reliability. The thinking being that if Tank 2 has a .999999 reliability rate, then when the .000001 happens, the other one should still be good. Probability on your side. Another branch on the tree. But probability assumes these are independent events. Whereas when Tank 1 is a few inches away from Tank 2, and Tank 2 blows up, the reliability of Tank 1 is suddenly going to be less than .999999. And we need Tank 1 to get home.

A response: garbled.

"*Odyssey*, *Aquarius*, say again, over."

I wait.

At last: "...still steady, Jim. I saw a fluctuation earlier, but right now we're OK."

It occurs to me that it's a good thing the explosion didn't happen earlier in the flight. If Tank 2 had been any fuller, the explosion might have knocked out Tank 1 as well.

"How are you on power?" Another concern. If the electricity isn't stable, we can't gimbal the SPS and do a proper burn. We'd be liable to end up tumbling. Or off course. Somewhere other than Earth.

"Fuel Cells 1 and 3 dropped offline…been able to restore 1. The spacecraft was rattled around a bit and I almost lost the alignment, but we are still OK." Ken sounds curt, businesslike. I'm glad he's up there. He knows the CSM better than anyone. "We need to keep the platform…so much debris I don't think I could do another alignment."

This is undoubtedly serious. They designed the guidance system with three gyroscopes. If you move into certain attitudes, they will lock up. Then you have to do another star alignment, otherwise you can't do an SPS burn to get home. And he's saying we can't do another alignment.

"Understood, *Odyssey*."

McCandless interjects: "Jim, we're not confident about the condition of the SPS, over."

In the space program, short sentences speak volumes. The SPS is the CSM's main engine. Our only ticket home. And because they couldn't make it redundant, they made it as reliable as possible. But there are a few failure modes. It's powered by hypergolics. Fuels that ignite on contact. So it's simple. But if the hydrazine and nitrogen tetroxide lines have been ruptured, we're in trouble. If the hypergolics come together outside the combustion chamber, there will be an explosion. Possibly far worse than what already happened. If the SPS doesn't work at all, we're stuck in lunar orbit until we run out of power and oxygen. If it doesn't work precisely, we're Lord knows where. Orbiting the sun, maybe. Lost in space.

In short, anything less than perfect will be fatal.

But there is no point dwelling on this. I look out at the stars and the perfect blackness in between. I am only thinking about what needs to be done. "Understood, Houston. Can we do anything about it?"

I wait for their answer.

At last: "We're working on that now, Jim."

●●●

I've rarely been afraid when out in nature. I understand the dangers in a theoretical sense. But emotionally I'm at peace. You look at the surface of the sea and the average person will let their mind run wild, conjuring up all the ways they can die. Storms, sinkings, sea serpents. I just see the sea.

I never realized until I went to space that I'd never really been in nature. Statistically speaking. What we see as normal is anything but. I think of the Greeks and their classical elements: fire, earth, air, water. When you are in orbit you see the great black space beyond all of this. The Greeks thought their four elements represented everything. They had no concept of zero. They couldn't know how much of everything is nothing. 99.999999% and on, to Lord knows how many decimal places. When you look at it that way, we are insignificant.

●●●

"Forward hatch closed and locked. Dump valve to auto," I tell everyone. We are doing a cabin repress and getting ready for liftoff. Taking comfort in routine.

"Breaker closed," Freddo says. "And the cabin is repressurizing."

From Houston: "Sounds good, *Aquarius.*"

"Pressure regulators A and B going to cabin. PLSS oxygen off."

"PLSS O2 is off," I echo.

"Let's go PTT," Freddo says.

In other words: Let's talk without everyone listening. "Going to PTT," I announce. Again I think of the astronauts talking in the pod in *2001.* Trying not to be overheard. Houston is our HAL. But they're trying to keep us alive.

"I'm not confident about the condition of the SPS," Freddo says.

"What choice do we have?"

"Do the mission. Go to Cone Crater."

"We'd still have the same issue tomorrow."

He shrugs.

Obviously we could, if we so choose, be the first humans to die on the moon. I don't know if this is what he's suggesting. Ordinarily it's not something either one of us would contemplate, but this is obviously not an ordinary situation.

(In the movies, I suppose there could be a real argument here. Tension, frustration, disagreement, shouting. But we're both adults. We both know the stakes. So what purpose would any of that serve? There's enough to be tense about without us adding to it.)

At last I reply: "When we were up here on 8, since we were gone on Christmas, I arranged to send Marilyn a fur coat with a note. 'Merry Christmas from the Man in the Moon.' Trying to make light of things. Because it was tense. Frank's wife was convinced, absolutely *convinced*, that the SPS would fail. That we'd be stranded in lunar orbit. And obviously none of us plans for failure. But one night I couldn't sleep. Not worried, just thinking. And it occurred to me: They'd probably take our wives in to the MOCR and let them say their goodbyes. And then we would have just turned the radios off."

Fred cocks his head.

"That way it'd all be hazy in their minds. If they wanted to, even years later, they could just look up at the moon and say, 'He's still up there.' Well, if we had a zero probability of return here, if the CSM crashed in front of us, that'd be one thing. But if that probability isn't zero, I wouldn't want my family thinking I'd done anything to minimize it. So as much as I want to see Cone Crater, I'm not gonna be the Man in the Moon."

Freddo nods. Or maybe it's a nod. I don't ask.

We're resetting a few circuit breakers and doffing our gloves when Houston comes on: "Jim, we're going to have Ken do a quick SPS burn at 10% thrust before we go LOS on the CSM. That should let us give you more data."

Another innocent sentence, heavy with meaning. They are going to test the main engine with a quick burn. If it blows up, our decision will be made for us. Do they know what we're thinking? Probably. It doesn't take a rocket scientist to figure it out, although obviously we have plenty on hand.

"I assume they've been discussing this in the back rooms."

"Roger, Jim. There was some talk about the risks of doing an extra burn. But we've looked at the telemetry and we think it'll be best all around. And unless you have any objections, we're gonna give it a go."

"If this is Flight's best decision, I'm fine with it."

We go back to stowing gear. The mass must be precisely distributed for a successful liftoff. There is a hanging spring scale like you would use for weighing a fish. We're supposed to be using it for boxes of moon rocks. We have none besides the contingency sample. But Houston also told us to keep our PLSS packs, which we ordinarily would have thrown out after the second EVA. We know the weights of some things already. But it is good to double-check. Maybe it's busywork, but it's something to do.

We hear Ken talking through the lead-up to the burn: "...Main B, Auto...Main A, Auto...AC2, off. BMAGS to 1 ATT, Spacecraft controller to SCS."

Neither Freddo nor I acknowledge it, but we both stop working to listen a little better.

"...getting some vibrations here," Ken says, crackly. "...unstable pitch gimbal. And...Master Alarm."

"Shut it down, Ken. We'll get as much data as we can before LOS."

"Fuel Cell 1 is back offline. We're back down to one...SPS just started oscillating."

"Roger, Ken. We might be able to do the burn with the secondary system."

"OK. Yaw 1's off, Pitch 1's off, Yaw 2's off, Pitch 2's off...Servos 1 and 2 are off...back to P00 so I can resolve the fuel cell issue."

"*Aquarius* is standing by," I radio.

"We copy, Jim," Houston says. "We will get you revised liftoff times."

More packing. Houston works their tracking magic and gives us the new numbers.

Things are settling down. Or maybe it just feels that way. It's still a crisis, but we have our bearings. We are working off of a surface abort checklist now. They have dreamed up a fair number of off-nominal contingency scenarios, so we aren't completely in the dark. This is what happens when thousands of people think about a particular set of problems for years on end.

And then, a transmission that makes us listen up: "Houston, *Odyssey*...levels on Tank 1 are acting up. They dropped after the burn and plateaued...just saw another drop."

"Roger, *Odyssey.* We're monitoring that. We'll have to take a look after AOS."

Freddo and I trade glances.

We get back to business as Ken heads behind the moon.

• • •

Like much of science, space exploration is a numbers game. Large numbers, small numbers. 218,096 nautical miles—the distance from the earth to the moon. 235 cubic feet—the interior volume of the LM cabin. 9,200 ft/s—the max delta-v of the SPS engine. There are high probabilities that somehow avoid you. There are low probabilities that catch up with you because you hang around them for too long. There is a small but non-zero probability that the LM will be struck by a micrometeorite large enough to rupture the hull while we're in it without our fishbowls on, in which case we'd be dead. And there is a large probability that the AGC will function without breaking for the entire course of a two-week mission. But it's still a number less than one.

The AGC handles large and small numbers much the same way you do when you use a slide rule. When you express a number in scientific notation you get two parts, the mantissa and the exponent. So 218,096 nautical miles becomes $2.18096 * 10^5$. You express everything in scientific notation and you perform all operations on the mantissas and then you use the exponent parts to determine where to put the decimal in your result. And that, of course, determines the significance of the number.

A key part of Kennedy's pledge was getting a man back to Earth safely. And several members of the Space Task Group (Bob Gilruth and Caldwell Johnson and Max Faget and a few others) had to determine what constituted "safely." They decided on a .99 probability of mission success. So, theoretically, one mission in a hundred will fail. And they settled on a probability of .999 for getting the crew back safely. So, in theory, one crew in a thousand will die.

The problem is you don't know, statistically, the actual probabilities of system failure. You can draw all the probability trees you want, but you won't know if the percentages are accurate unless you test each component thousands of times. And since that's not going to happen, you won't really know if the overall probability is correct unless you fly a thousand missions. And one in a thousand doesn't sound like a lot, until you're the one.

I guess what I'm saying is: it's all a question of significance. Move the decimal point too far one way and everything starts to look like nothing. Move it too much the other way and nothing becomes everything.

Obviously no one knows everything that's happened deep inside the CSM. Which systems are just hanging on until the next vibration. What will happen if we do a full burn. The SPS might be fine except for a loose connection to the gimbal motor. Or it could be about to explode. They are working to get as complete a picture as possible, but we won't be able to do much besides make better decisions. This isn't like the movies where the hero can do a dramatic spacewalk and fix everything and save the mission. Our engines were designed for reliability, not maintenance. Simple, self-contained structures filled with extremely caustic propellants that would probably eat through our gloves. So we're stuck with what we've got. The SPS will either give us enough delta-v to get us home, or it won't. It's up there in some indeterminate state. Like Schrödinger's thought experiment where the cat is simultaneously alive and dead until you open the box. A cloud of probabilities ready to collapse into one reality. Only we're the cat. And we won't know our end state until we light the SPS again.

I suppose I can understand, in a theoretical sense, why some people would choose to just stay on the moon in those circumstances. To spend a final day or so exploring, and say their goodbyes, and turn off the radios. But I wouldn't be in this spot in the first place if I was that type of person. And I hope the same goes for Freddo.

During that last bit of work everything fades away except what is in front of us. Neither of us is looking out the window. The surface of the moon might be 99.999999% uninhabited and airless right now, but we are going to do what we can on our little slice of it.

•••

"Odyssey, Houston. Come in. Over."

We can't help listening a little. Waiting with bated breath. Ken should be coming back around. But: no answer.

Again: "Odyssey, Houston. Come in. Over."

At last: "Houston, Odyssey. Still here. Over."

They ask our question for us: "What is the condition of the O2 tank? Over."

"It is...steady for now."

Brief relief. But then: "Do you think it'll hold up for TEI?"

"Well, that is the $64,000 question. But it's safe to say I'm not brimming with confidence. Over."

"Copy, Odyssey."

We get back to work. We will not know until it happens.

•••

And now we are almost at liftoff.

"*Aquarius,* Houston, you can take Descent Battery 2 off now."

"OK, Houston." Freddo flips the switch.

The way it works is the bottom part of the spacecraft, the descent stage, becomes the launch pad for the top half. We tested the ascent-stage batteries a while back but have been running down the descent batteries as long as possible because everything in that stage has to stay on the moon. There is a lot of oxygen in there that we can't take with us. I am not complaining. They designed it the way it needed to be designed. I wouldn't have done it any differently, even now.

We've done what we can. We even topped off the PLSS packs with O2 from the descent stage. Given the overall consumables need for the three of us on the way home, it may not make a difference. Still, there's a chance a few extra hours' worth of oxygen will come in handy.

In the meantime, Houston has been working through revised procedures for our TEI burn. Calculating probabilities for longer burns at lower thrust. Trying to change mantissas and lower exponents in a way that raises probabilities.

But at the end of all that there is no certainty.

"Aquarius, Houston. It's your call now, Jim."

"OK, Houston." But there is no decision. "We are standing by to pressurize the ascent helium."

A simple system: no pumps, just gas forcing propellant to the engine. Very little to break. But you can only pressurize it right before launch. Otherwise the pressure will eventually bleed off and you will have no way to fire the engine or steer. So this is it. Once we do this, we will not be able to delay the rest of it.

I look over. Freddo is looking out the window at the bleak bright scene.

I don't think he's thinking of anything other than getting one last look. Which is understandable. Still I say: "There's nothing for us down here, Freddo."

He doesn't say anything.

Houston: "Go ahead, *Aquarius*. One at a time, please."

Freddo reaches for the switch. If he hesitates, I don't see it. "There's Number 1, Houston."

We watch the pressure gauges climb.

Freddo flips another switch. "OK, there's Number 2."

There is a pause while we wait for the final GO. Now we are both getting a last look. Neither of us says anything.

At last, a crackle. "*Aquarius*, this is Houston. You are GO for lift-off this pass. Direct rendezvous. Guidance control: PGNS. Over."

"Roger, Houston. Go for lift-off. Direct rendezvous. PGNS. Over."

A pause. Then: "Godspeed, *Aquarius*."

We have some final circuit breaker changes, per pages 8-16 and 8-17 of the surface checklist. And now we have to go to VHF for a comm check with *Odyssey*. Ken is nearly overhead. We will need to talk to him real-time to do the rendezvous.

"*Odyssey*, *Aquarius*, how do you read?"

I wait.

"*Odyssey*, *Aq…*"

A faint voice. "Jim, I read you. Not perfect, but it'll have to do."

"OK, Ken, we have you about 3 by," I respond. "Two minutes to liftoff...mark."

"*Aquarius*, Houston. Less than two minutes and we are GO."

More switches. There are pyrotechnic systems in the descent stage that fire guillotines that sever the electrical and plumbing connections between the two stages. "Master Arm is on. A and B lights are on."

From Houston: "Roger, *Aquarius*, we confirm both systems armed." And to Ken: "*Odyssey*, Houston, *Aquarius* has ascent engine armed."

"Roger, Houston, I am reading them loud and clear now."

"OK, Ken, we'll be up there shortly," I say.

A quick scan of the DSKY. Our clock's counting down. Everything looks right. This is happening.

"Ten, nine, eight...Abort Stage set. Engine Arm," I call out, and the explosive bolts and guillotines fire and the DSKY is flashing 99 and Freddo pushes PRO. "Proceed," he calls out, and I continue "...four, three, two, one."

And the engine lights and Freddo calls: "Ignition." And the floor presses against us and I look out the window in time to catch a quick glimpse of a flurry of torn Mylar skittering across the lunar surface, which is quickly falling away.

"Velocity's good, and we have pitchover," I call out as the eight-balls roll again and the LM pitches forward.

We have to build horizontal velocity to catch up to the CSM. So, unlike on the way in, we're looking down at the moon. And we're swaying a little as the RCS fires. And I am busy tracking values against printed cue cards, but it occurs to me how strange this is. And I keep scanning the instruments to make sure the computer's doing what it's supposed to do, but once or twice I look out at the craters below. And the dead landscape whips by, faster and faster and faster.

•••

On Apollo 11 and 12, they executed a conservative rendezvous technique. Coelliptic. Basically a slower ascent with several burns along the way to refine the LM's trajectory. Rendezvous three and a half hours after liftoff.

But Apollo means gradual improvements. New capabilities from mission to mission. Never getting too far ahead of yourself, but always going forward. So our planners pushed for a direct rendezvous. Fewer burns, faster link-up with the CSM. And given the current crisis, we have all the more reason to get up there quicker.

The initial ascent places us in an orbit 9 nautical miles at its lowest point and 45 at its highest. From there, it's one big burn to close the gap.

•••

During the first hour after orbital insertion, we are flying through the moon's shadow. Launched into lunar night. A bisected universe. Everything above: innumerable stars and galaxies. And nothing below but cold dark blankness. I saw it on Apollo 8 and before we landed on this mission, and it still gives me chills.

In this phase, we can't see *Odyssey*. We have to track him with the rendezvous radar. Making sure everyone's where they're supposed to be. Trusting in the unseen.

Terminal Phase Insertion takes place after crossing the lunar terminator. Another crucial burn. Talking to Ken on the VHF but still out of contact with Houston. Now that we are out of the moon's shadow and aligned properly I can see the cloud of oxygen around the CSM. It's flecked with pieces of debris that drift slowly and glint as they catch the sun.

"Oh, Lord, that's quite a cloud," I say.

A crackling transmission. "*...quarius*, *Odyssey*, say again, over."

"That's quite a cloud you've got around you, Ken. But I will say, it's easy to get a visual when you're surrounded by debris."

"Always look on the bright side, huh?" Ken says.

I steal a glimpse at this bright slice of the far side. A much different view of the moon than most humans see. None of the dark lowlands. I will only see it twice more, and never after today.

"*Aquarius*, Houston, how do you read, over?" Houston calls us up after AOS.

"We're here, Houston. TPI was nominal and everybody's where they're supposed to be."

A crackle. "...you have the numbers, *Aquarius*?"

Freddo reads them off: "Noun 81, plus 62.1, plus 0.1, plus 63.1. The burn went on time. We nulled PGNS to 00 plus 0.1."

"We have sight of *Odyssey* and it is a fair-sized cloud orbiting with them," I add.

"Roger, *Aquarius*. *Odyssey*, how's it working from your end?"

"Well, the sextant was pretty much useless. But I was able to pick up a VHF range after TPI, and I saw their strobe once we were in range for that."

"Roger, *Odyssey*," Houston calls. Then: "*Aquarius*, take your time on the way in. We'd like to have Fred get some pictures of the CSM."

"We'll see what we can do, Houston."

"And *Odyssey*, you were able to get the LM weight of 5600 pounds loaded into the DAP?"

"Roger, Houston," Ken answers. He had to get our weight entered into his computer so the autopilot functions properly once we're docked. Despite the crisis, we still have to check all the boxes.

The CSM is obviously in bad shape. We ease our way in close. Then Ken does a quick RCS rotation to put the damaged side of the spacecraft in front of us.

Freddo and I both gasp.

"Houston, *Aquarius*, there's a whole side of the spacecraft missing. The entire panel appears to have been blown off. We can see in along that shelf, and Tank 2 is completely gone."

"Roger, *Aquarius*. What is the condition of the SPS, over?"

"Houston, the SPS appears to be in good shape. I do see a streak along the engine bell that I didn't see before."

"Roger, *Aquarius*." Houston sounds more distant than ever. "Use your best judgment and get all the pictures you can."

Fred's taking care of that, working the 70mm Hasselblad. He spends a roll shooting the side of the spacecraft. These photos should be a huge help to whatever accident board they convene to determine what happened to us. Provided, of course, we can take them back to get developed.

The docking itself is surprisingly uneventful. There was some talk of us taking the active role for the final link-up, but Ken has stabilized things to the point that he's comfortable with *Odyssey* handling this. And we have to be careful so we don't go into gimbal lock and lose our alignment.

"Apollo 13, Houston, you are GO for docking."

I watch through the overhead window as the CSM moves toward us for the last couple minutes. A smooth approach, particularly given the circumstances. Moving together so that speed and distance both go to zero at the same time.

"We have capture," Ken calls out before I'm sure I've even felt anything. And then: "We have a hard dock."

We hear the ripple of the latches engaging. It's somewhat reassuring. Whatever our other problems, some things are working normally.

•••

After the docking, Ken has to remove the nose probe assembly and equalize the pressure so he can open up the tunnel between the two spacecraft.

Ordinarily we would be unstowing boxes of moon rocks and getting ready to transfer them over. Instead, Houston reads a revised checklist. We are transferring over the PLSS packs, and a few nylon tethers so we can stow them under the couches for the reentry we're hoping to have three days from now. It goes without saying that none of us knows if any of this will make a difference. If we're close to reentry and the tank fails, the extra oxygen might mean everything. If the tank fails now, we're just delaying our deaths. Still, it beats doing nothing.

We pull up some guidance numbers from the DSKY in *Aquarius* and read them through the tunnel to Ken so he can convert them and plug them in to *Odyssey*. Meanwhile Ken has reconfigured circuits and breakers to draw some power from *Aquarius* while we're still attached.

After that, a long burn with the LM attitude thrusters until they're nearly spent. Something Houston cooked up to give us a touch more delta-v and cut down on the burden on the SPS later. It's awkward flying, trying to steer the whole stack from the little LM. Like backing a boat trailer down a ramp. We've never simulated anything remotely like it.

And at last we are back in the CSM. Houston reads up a pad for us to jettison the ascent stage of the LM. Its trajectory will cause it to impact the moon in a way that will be picked up by the seismometers they left during Apollo 12. There haven't been many opportunities for science on this mission, but we're doing what we can.

Soon we're closed out and Houston has given us a GO for jettison.

"The end of the age of *Aquarius*," Ken says as he presses the button.

"Fare thee well," I add, as if the LM cares what we think.

I do feel a bit sad watching it get smaller in the window. Throwing away something that was working perfectly fine for the sake of something broken. But it is time. The LM was perfect for when we needed it, and we took what we could from it, and now it's perfectly useless.

"All right, I've got a TEI-21 pad for you, in case you're interested," Houston calls up.

Trans-Earth Injection. The instructions for the burn to get home. In case we're interested. I chuckle.

Ken speaks: "Yeah, that might be useful."

"Let me know when you're ready to copy."

"Pen in hand, Houston."

"TEI-21, SPS G&N 34620. Minus 0.72, plus 0.08 129:18:05.29. NOUN 81: Plus 3013.3, Plus 1667.4, Minus 0340.3. Attitude: 180,000,000. NOUN 44: HA, N/A. HP, Plus 0019.0; 3460.6, 2:28, 3436.6. No sextant stars, but we will read up a pad so you can do a coarse align with Earth. Ullage, 4 jets, 12 seconds. Go ahead with your readback, over."

Ken has been scribbling furiously and now he recites it all flawlessly from his notes. Noun 81 gives the delta-v we want from the burn. Noun 44 is Apolune and Perilune. High and low points for the orbit after the burn. But of course the high point is Earth.

Like all TEI burns, this has to happen on the far side. Out of radio contact. Out of sight of Earth.

I suppose it's just as well. In this business, we can't get anything done without Houston's help. But at the end of the day we are each on our own to meet our fate. The best anyone else can ever do is hold your hand.

Houston reads back expected times for AOS. They'll be back in touch with us at 129:28:35 if the burn goes according to plan, and about ten minutes later if it doesn't happen at all. (And given the fragile state of the SPS and the explosivity of the hypergolics, there is a third option. No more CSM, no AOS. But obviously there's no point dwelling on that.)

And finally we are heading for our last LOS. We do a coarse alignment check by maneuvering the CSM so that the earth is visible through the sextant, because it's about the only thing we're able to see through the optics. Then another alignment check to see the earth through the commander's window.

I suppose you might be wondering if I'm regretting anything that led to this point. If I would have done anything differently. Well, I can say whatever I want, but ultimately it doesn't matter. Obviously I can say I'm eager to get home to my wife and kids, but it's useless to wish I'd never left. We are here. Today's decisions are the only ones that matter.

I will say that I appreciate the earth in a way that someone who's never left it can't fully understand. When I first saw *2001,* I was baffled by the ending shots. Particularly the fetus floating in space. But I kept thinking about it. And now it makes sense. On this scale, the entire scope of human life is fragile to the point of insignificance. And yet it is also everything.

Before our orbit takes us behind the moon, we rotate the spacecraft into the proper attitude for the burn. Command module facing ahead, SPS pointing backwards. We do not see Earth set behind us.

And then, alone in the dark over the far side, we wait. Everything is keyed in. We scan the electrolumescent instruments. Everything is obviously not normal, but everything is as expected. The spacecraft speeds ahead, but we have no sense of motion. The clock ticks down relentlessly. Our only proof life hasn't stopped.

In a minute it will all be resolved. Ken is letting me do the honors. Like with the lunar descent burn in the LM, I will have to wait until the timer gets below five seconds, and the computer will flash 99, asking for confirmation, and I will tell it to go ahead. And all the hazy percentages will solidify. Will turn into ones and zeroes. All the branches will fall from the probability tree, save one: the crooked ugly path that got us here.

"And we've had ullage," I say, as the RCS fires to settle the propellant in its tanks. "Ten, nine, eight..." I call out, although only Ken and Fred can hear me.

The clock ticks down.

The numbers flash.

I press the button.

PRO. Proceed.

ACKNOWLEDGMENTS

I'm tremendously grateful to Apollo 13's commander, Captain James Lovell, USN (Ret.) for his help in the preparation of this manuscript. He was gracious enough to provide answers to several of my questions; though terse, his answers were also pithy and illuminating, and helped me better understand the types of men who went to the moon. His commentary on the finished manuscript also provided much-needed encouragement for me to take the relatively insignificant risk of getting it out there.

I'm also very indebted to Apollo 14's Captain Edgar Mitchell, USN (Ret.), PhD, for taking time out of his schedule for a phone interview. The sixth person to walk on the moon, and the only remaining astronaut to have visited the Fra Mauro Highlands, Dr. Mitchell took the time to talk to me about something he's been talking about for over half his life, and that in turn helped make this a more credible and convincing story.

Primary sources are history's lifeblood, and since the six Apollo moon landings are among the most documented events in human existence, there's an abundance of them available via NASA's websites. However, they wouldn't have made nearly as much sense if not for the stellar (pun intended) work done by Eric Jones and the astronauts he interviewed for the Lunar Surface Journal. This manuscript would have been nowhere near as accurate without that resource, which is invaluable for any serious student of Apollo. In addition, he was gracious enough to answer several tricky technical questions I had, to provide commentary and feedback on my first draft of the manuscript, and to catch several technical errors.

Giano Cromley is a fantastic and talented author, and it has been my great pleasure to have him as a travel companion for the physically safe (but emotionally treacherous) journey into the uncharted space of independent publishing. His feedback on this manuscript was extremely helpful, and he also caught several errors that would have been disastrously embarrassing.

Special thanks to Lauren Boegen, Digital Collections Manager at the Adler Planetarium, for obtaining permission to edit their historical photograph of Apollo 13's cuff checklist. In the interest of historical accuracy, the original image of the actual cuff checklist is included here:

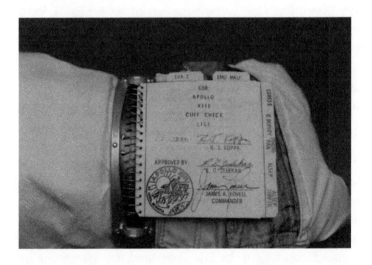

The Adler Planetarium was also very gracious in providing photographs of Jim Lovell's LEVA helmet for my cover art.

Nick Bianco of Nick Bianco Photography did a wonderful job of editing the cover photograph.

Many thanks to Francis French for his enthusiasm and support, and for spotting what I hope was the last remaining typo.

Dr. Andrew Chaikin's *A Man on the Moon* rekindled my interest in Apollo several years ago, and remains the single best book on the subject; it's the next best thing to taking six trips to the moon. David A. Mindell's *Digital Apollo* and Frank O'Brien's *The Apollo Guidance Computer: Architecture and Operation* were both awesome resources on the design and behavior of Apollo's computers. *Apollo* by Charles Murray and Catherine Bly Cox is perhaps the best book on the unglamorous (read *non-astronaut*) side of Apollo, and the hard-working and anonymous thousands who put a famous few on the lunar surface. Gene Kranz's *Failure is Not an Option* also gave a much needed glimpse into the lives and work of those men and women who worked in NASA's control rooms. Jim Lovell and Jeffrey Kluger's *Lost Moon/Apollo 13* is a gripping space adventure that also captures many technical details about Apollo 13's voyage. Dr. Edgar Mitchell's *The Way of the Explorer* provided an intriguing look at his voyages, and also at his unconventional but thought-provoking dyadic model of the universe. *Carrying the Fire* by Michael Collins remains the best firsthand account by any of the Apollo astronauts; it's a remarkably delightful read. (If NASA had deliberately recruited an author to ride along on a moon mission, they still couldn't have produced a better book.) Though not about Apollo, Mike Mullane's *Riding Rockets* is one of the best and most enjoyable astronaut memoirs ever written, and a great look at their mindset. Buzz Aldrin's *Magnificent Desolation* was an interesting and worthwhile read, and a much-needed reminder that worldly and otherworldly triumph isn't the end-all be-all of life. *Into that Silent Sea* and *In the Shadow of the Moon* by Francis French and Colin

Burgess were both great and compelling books about the early years of space exploration. Francis French and Al Worden's *Falling to Earth* was also a very worthwhile contribution to the Apollo literature. Thomas Kelly's *Moon Lander* details the Lunar Module's construction and sophisticated engineering, as well as the trials and tribulations of those who turned that engineering into reality. And the anonymous contributors to Wikipedia continue to ensure that their site remains a handy quick and generally very reliable reference, at least on matters like this.

Last, but by far not least, Octavia and Genesis continue to be the best family anyone could ask for; they make all my voyages far less appealing, and my returns home far more enjoyable.

About the Author

Mr. Brennan earned a B.S. in European History from the United States Military Academy at West Point and an M.S. in Journalism from Columbia University in New York. His writing has appeared in the *Chicago Tribune*, *The Good Men Project*, and *Innerview Magazine*; he's also been a frequent contributor and co-editor at Back to Print and <u>The Deadline.</u> He resides in Chicago.

Follow him on Twitter @jerry_brennan.

About Tortoise Books

Slow and steady wins in the end, even in publishing. Tortoise Books is dedicated to finding and promoting quality authors who haven't yet found a niche in the marketplace—writers producing memorable and engaging works that will stand the test of time.

Learn more at www.tortoisebooks.com, or follow us on Twitter @TortoiseBooks.

9 780998 632506